a minedition book

North American edition published 2015 by Michael Neugebauer Publishing Ltd. Hong Kong

First published in German 1990 by Beltz Verlag, Weinheim und Basel
Original title: Das Tier mit den Funkelaugen
Text copyright © 2014 Annelies Schwarz
Illustrations copyright © 2014 Kveta Pacovská
English text translation by the publisher
Rights arranged with "minedition" Rights and Licensing AG, Zurich, Switzerland.

Michael Neugebauer Publishing Ltd., Unit 23, 7F, Kowloon Bay Industrial Centre,
15 Wang Hoi Road, Kowloon Bay, Hong Kong.
e-mail: info@minedition.com
This book was printed in May 2015 at L.Rex Printing Co Ltd.,
3/F., Blue Box Factory Building, 25 Hing Wo Street, Tin Wan, Aberdeen, Hong Kong, China
Typesetting in Kabel
Color separation by Pixelstorm, Vienna
Library of Congress Cataloging-in-Publication Data available upon request.

ISBN 978-988-8240-47-0

10 9 8 7 6 5 4 3 2 1
First Impression

For more information please visit our website: www.minedition.com

Annelies Schwarz
Květa Pacovská

MY BEDTIME MONSTER

minedition

Rikki wishes she had a pet.
"My pet should be soft and cuddly," she says,
"and also quick and strong. It should be able to
fly, so I can ride it across the sky. And it should
be able to swim, so that we could dive beneath
the waves."

But that isn't all. "I wish I had a pet that could
shrink so small, it could hide anywhere," she says,
"and one that could grow so big it could protect me."

"There is no such pet,"
her mother tells her.
"I've never seen an animal like that,"
her father says.
"I'll bet you I'm right!"
Rikki proclaims with a yawn
as she climbs into bed.

The next thing Rikki knows she… well,
she doesn't know quite where she is.
A voice calls to her as she lies in bed.
Look for me!
Rikki perks up her ears in the darkness.
Look for me!
Rikki scans carefully at the foot of the bed,
where she spies—
"There you are, I've found you!" she shouts,
nearly grabbing the soft creature.

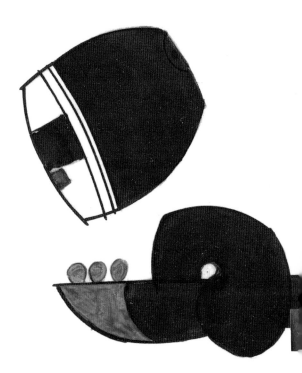

"Now catch me!" it calls to her, rushing across the room,
jumping over the bed, the dresser, and the table.
Rikki springs out of bed and chases after it.
The creature crouches near the toys, and Rikki can see its
sparkling eyes.
With a leap she captures the creature and holds on tight.

"Now let's fight!" says the creature.

It grows and grows until it's a giant monster.
Rikki's heart beats faster, full of excitement.
The two wrestle each other until Rikki is exhausted.

"Now let's fly!" the monster says.

Rikki watches as the monster sprouts a pair
of broad and beautiful wings.
"Come on!" the monster says.
Together they launch out above the garden.

"Hang on tight, we'll zoom even higher!"

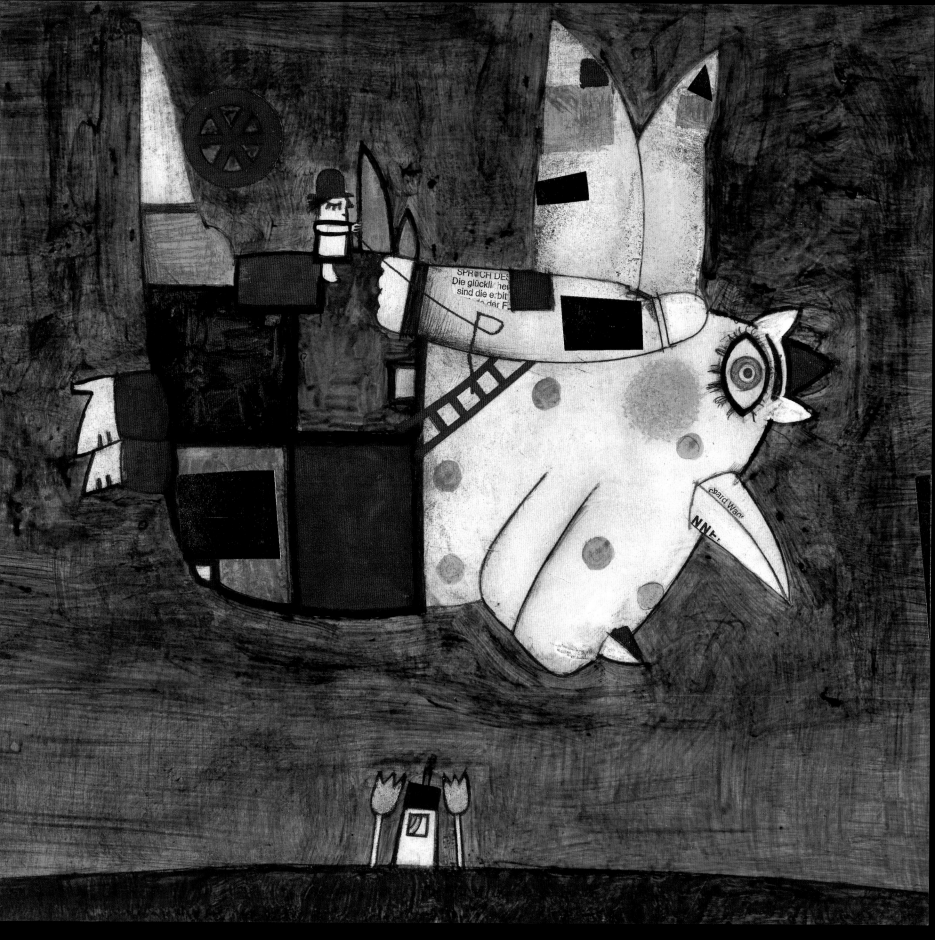

Rikki holds on as the monster
soars with her through the night.
"Watch out!" Rikki shouts,
"the tall chimney…"
They swerve around it just in
time, and Rikki thinks:
Don't fall off now!
"Close your eyes," the monster
calls, "and get ready to dive!"

Before Rikki realizes it they're underwater.
She opens her eyes to see that she's now riding
an enormous fish. They swim past clams and
seaweed until they find a dark cave.
"Make yourself small now," Rikki says.

Rikki wants to see what's hidden in the cave. Her creature shrinks down to become a tiny fish, and Rikki shrinks down with it, too. They slip through the cave's entrance. But what's this? A huge mouth is opening before them. It's a nasty sea ogre!

"Quick, quick," Rikki shouts, "let's grow again!"

Rikki is scared they'll be swallowed, but quicker than quick,
Rikki and her monster grow so big that when the ogre snaps
his mouth shut there's nothing there anymore.
The ogre wonders: *Wasn't something just here?*
Or have I already swallowed it?

"Good job, my pet!" Rikki says, laughing as they glide gently
 through the water.
 Then they see a broad, bright stripe in front of them.
"What's that?" Rikki asks.
"That's the moonlight," Rikki's pet answers.
"We must turn back now. We've gone a long way from home."

With a mighty swing of its fin, the monster turns around, and swims with Rikki up to the surface.

As soon as they reach the shore, the monster's mane and tail have returned. It stretches and jumps through the air.

Snuggled up on the monster's back, Rikki and her pet make their way home.
From a distance Rikki can see her house. The window of her room is wide open.

Together they touch down on the carpet in front of Rikki's bed.
"Stay with me, please, and always protect me," Rikki says, beginning to
yawn again.
"Of course I will," her monster says.
It sits guard over Rikki for the rest of the night.

The next morning Rikki jumps out of bed and runs to her mother.

"My perfect pet does exist!" she announces gleefully.

"Where is it?" Rikki's mother asks in surprise.

"You can't see it now, of course," Rikki answers,

"it has made itself too small."

"Is that so?" Rikki's mother asks with a wink.

Then she takes hold of Rikki's hand and says,

"Come on, let's start the day."

Born in Bohemia, in the Czech Republic, **Annelies Schwarz** has been a teacher, a drama instructor, a writer, and a painter. She leads creative artists programs all over the world, and has written more than 30 books for children, including international award-winners. She lives and works at her studio on the coast of the North Sea.

Květa Pacovská was born in Prague in 1928. She studied painting and illustration at the Prague College of Fine Arts, and it was there that she first encountered avant-garde European art. Throughout her career she has drawn inspiration from its famous figures and their aesthetic preferences: influences on her artistic career and her personal development have been Paul Klee, Vassily Kandinsky, and Joan Miró, as well as the Bauhaus artists. Her work shows great diversity. In the last 40 years she has published over 75 books, and at least 100 national and international exhibitions have been devoted to her works of art. They range from painting, graphic art, and collage, to objects made of paper. In this way she experiments with a new link between text and image.

In 1992 she received the Hans Christian Andersen Medal, the highest international distinction in literature for young people, for her lifetime achievement in art, and in 1993 she received the Lettre d'Argent, one of the highest awards for book illustration.